PURE
SLUSH
BOOKS

Vestal Aversion

a month of stories

Matt Potter

Vestal Aversion (second edition)
published by Pure Slush, September 2014.

Pure Slush Books
4 Warburton Street
Magill SA 5072
Australia

ISBN: 978—1—925101—94—2

Find *Pure Slush* at http://pureslush.webs.com

Copies of all *Pure Slush* publications can be bought
at http://pureslush.webs.com/store.htm

All queries re *Pure Slush* can be made
via email to edpureslush@live.com.au

for
Sweets Crippen,
international film star
and an early favourite

Contents

~

Sharp

Shiny

Introduction

~

Hmm, another book with a snappy title that sounds great but is actually not connected to the book's meaning ... ?

Yes, I would think the same.

And what does the cover have to do with anything?

Well, I was living in Berlin, had experienced one writers' group run by a man who was confused about most things – especially about how to communicate effectively – and then went to another, coaxed there by writers I'd met at the first group.

At this second group I was lucky to meet Marcus Speh – and this group was far far better – who introduced me to the world of flash fiction, and online publishing, and my world changed. Not only did it get me back into writing again – a lot – but I realised all those great ideas and moments and scenes I'd been storing for years now had a place to flower.

So now it's almost two years later and *Vestal Aversion* is in your hands. I hope you enjoy it, as much as I did creating these memorable moments (!).

Matt Potter,
May 2012

Short

Old haggis

~

"You smell like old haggis, Dougal," he said, inserting the needle. I watched the vial fill with my dark blood. It made me think of colour swatches and shopping for just the right red tartan with my mother in an Edinburgh kilt shop.

"Thank you," I said. "I've been eating it a lot lately."

Odd, for at the time I was extremely yellow and not remotely haggis−like. But then, it was Berlin and the vagaries of the German health system were still largely unexplained to me.

"Herr Doktor Krumme," I said. "It's great that you do this every day. I would be lost without you."

He smiled as he withdrew the needle, replacing it with a cotton ball and some gentle pressure. Such service − other patients had to make do with nurses, but every day Doktor Krumme took my blood himself.

"And every day your liver count becomes a little less high." He smiled, gently pressing a plaster into the crook of my elbow.

"Well, I always like a good project," I said. I got up out of the chair and running the grim glare of Frau Renntner as she sentried behind the reception desk, walked to my tent in the waiting room.

I tried to like Frau Renntner. But her hostile stare and indiscriminate caber−tossing of my medical file into the compactus when Doktor Krumme wasn't looking, left little doubt in my mind about her lack of empathy.

Even when I offered her a slice of the Highland game pie I'd cooked from scratch on the camp stove beside her workstation, Frau Renntner still gave me the cold shoulder.

Lucky Doktor Krumme was so professional with his care.

I sat inside the entrance to my tent while other patients sitting in the waiting room read magazines or kept watch out of the corner of their eye. And as I tried to decide what to make for dinner that evening, flicking through the 'Recovering from Hepatitis A' cookbook – complete with legible inscription inside the front cover from Doktor Krumme himself – Doktor Krumme crouched beside me on the floor.

"Dougal," he said. "I think it will be better if I sleep here at night with you in this tent."

"Is there a problem with Security?" I asked. "Because I can learn to operate the alarm system. They don't have to be bothered every time I need the toilet."

Doktor Krumme smiled and patted my knee. "It will give us a time to get to know each other better." He squeezed my shoulder. "And you can cook for me on your camp stove your world–famous Scottish shortbread."

I looked into Doktor Krumme's face and saw more than just the Hippocratic oath: I saw love. So I guessed that night was as good a time as any to tell him I was faking my liver count too.

Meeting Adjourned

~

Once a month I fuck the boss. It's not part of my job description. We have a meeting in her office, after thirty minutes she opens the door to what appears to be a storeroom but is actually a well–appointed fuck chamber, and we adjourn.

She likes being fucked on her back mostly: she enjoys watching me do all the grunt work. I grind and groan, looking into her chemically–peeled face as she grips my arse, the fingers of her wrinkling hands edging towards my tightened hole – the storeroom is soundproofed, the door to her office triple–locked, though no one would dare enter without her permission anyway – and not much is said beyond "Deeper" and "Harder" and "Faster", all by her.

I don't believe she has a similar relationship with any of my work colleagues. And if she does, I don't care much either.

And if work colleagues heard of my 'relationship' with her, no one would believe it. I think she sees her conquest of me as a triumph of her supreme sexuality, her female carnality, or if nothing else, her economic power.

Thirty minutes before we meet, I take half a Viagra. I also jerk off three times earlier in the day, so by the time of our meeting, I'm trigger–hard and my balls are empty but ready to churn. I don't come inside her. She can't check: she's too old to get pregnant and we don't use condoms, so there's no inspection of the reservoir afterwards. But I give a good show. My legs and arse tense, I stop mid-thrust – like cresting a hill – then I push deep down inside her and moan. Maybe my face turns slightly red.

I make sure I fake my orgasm after I've made her come twice. She then wraps herself in a thick Egyptian cotton robe, opens a bread hamper, plugs in a Tefal toaster and makes two slices of toast with margarine and Vegemite. She never offers me any. I watch her eat off a white-grey Royal Copenhagen plate, bitch-red fingernails stabbing the wholemeal crumbs as she licks them clean. Enthusiasm almost lights her face.

She puts her plate on the low table beside the bed, sips her Powerjuice from a crystal tumbler – she only offers me iced tea: I always refuse as I loathe the taste, which I am sure she knows – and resumes talking.

"We're marketing ourselves into non-existence," she said one day, running her fingers through her messy, re-blonded crewcut. She spoke exactly as she would at our weekly Marketing Team meetings, to all the overpaid, over-airbrushed, hyper-hyped-up hipsters she'd assembled to make her and the products we sell look good.

"Callie Crawford Cosmetics is such an exclusive brand now, no one thinks they can afford to buy my products."

"I think you're right, Callie," I said, my tongue metaphorically twisting inside her arse. "We've marketed ourselves into a corner."

I know other staff call me Tom the tongue-twister. They know – or think they know – how far my tongue is up her arse. (This is one thing I have never done. Callie, despite our sessions in the over-sized cupboard, is a conventional lay.)

"I've let you all convince me your over-exclusive branding would give us an even bigger market share and now you've left us no room to move."

I sank against the plush pillow and looked at her profile: a largish nose, heavily mascara—ed lashes, lipstick that even in the storeroom light I could see was only half—chewed off.

"Reposition the brand," I said.

Her head turned on the pillow. Her lips curled: smile or sneer, I couldn't tell. "You must be fucking joking."

I looked at the ceiling.

"I've spent thirty years building this brand to where it is now."

"So, it'll be a challenge," I said, turning on my side away from her. I patted the pillow beside my head.

She punched my bare shoulder with the side of her fist. "Don't fucking turn away from me! Tell me what you mean."

"I told you," I said, sleep in my voice. "Reposition the brand."

"There's nowhere to go but down." I imagined her looking at my shoulder, eyes working overtime trying to fathom what I meant.

"Yeah," I said. "Reposition the brand at the bottom of the market and work your way up again." I looked at her over my shoulder. "If anyone can do it, you can."

Her hand rested on the spot where moments earlier she'd thumped me.

"It'd be dumbing the brand down."

"You'd make industry history and get more than your Albert Einstein fifteen minutes of fame," I said, hitting her at her greatest chink, her need to leave a legacy.

She sank back on her pillow and with her hand still on my shoulder, drummed her fingers like a metronome.

I pressed my head further into the pillow. I made my breathing deeper, each breath longer, eyes half—closed, but ears alert.

"It's a bullshit idea," Callie said, taking her hand away.

Through my eyelashes, I focussed on the weave of the cotton pillowslip, and paused before responding. "Start with the perfumes."

"And what would we call them? The names we have now are so high–end."

I thought of Callie's emotional depth.

"*Shallow,*" I said.

I thought of the folds of her vagina.

"*Umbrella,*" I added.

And I thought of the way I too often feel about her.

"*Omen* and *Death,*" I finished. "What slapper wouldn't want to wear a perfume called *Death*? Packaging would be cheaper and you'd sell it by the truckload. In fact, you could probably sell it off the back of a truck."

I stopped and listened to her breathing, shallow gasps every few seconds, as if denying herself air made her stronger. If I was a bastard, I'd say breathing and thinking at the same time were too taxing for her. But I'm not that much of a bastard.

"No one but you would have the balls to do it," I said.

Callie laughed. "It's a fucking amazing idea."

"Yeah, it is."

She whistled through her teeth. "Same scent, make a lot more of it, save on cost, just shift it differently."

"Yes, it's a brilliant idea."

Callie laughed again, and suddenly threw back the sheet. "Just remember who's paying you," she said. "And just so you realise, I know you never come inside me. It might be an old twat but it still has some feeling."

I reached down to the foot of the bed and slowly pulled the sheet back over me. Callie picked up her plate.

"You want some toast and Vegemite?" she said. "I think you need to tell me some more about this *incredible* idea."

That night, Callie went home to husband number four and I went home to my partner. The effect of the half a Viagra had not worn off, and I was soon lost in fucking Mario as, gripping my

20

arse, fingers edging towards my receptive hole, he yelled out *Deeper! Harder! Faster!* in a more genuine way, despite the lack of sound−proofing.

Sydney Hotel Room

~

The sensor light switches on as I pull into the driveway. I ratchet the handbrake, open the door, grab the gifts and step out into the evening air.

Moving towards the back door, I hear squeals of delight from the open bathroom window. The evening bathtime ritual is in full swing.

I looked at him, lying on the bed, lolling cock spent.

Then turned back to the mirror to knot my tie. I saw the forty–two year old wrinkles around my mouth and the world's longest mid–life crisis (five years) etched onto my expanding forehead.

I wouldn't do this again, I'd said. But then came the text message.

"How was the meeting?" my wife says, her arm folding into mine and kissing me on the lips, gifts on the countertop for later.

"Okay," I say, wondering if she smells traces of my real meeting. And smelling her own sweetness too. "Sales are bad, everything's too expensive, the future looks terrible."

"So, the usual." She smiles, brushing what's left of my hair off my forehead. "You look tired." She kisses me again and slips her tongue inside.

What I want is for him to really look at me and say, I love you.

But David has Gerhard and still loves him, even after twelve years. Even though their relationship feels more like brothers. Even though I've lost count of the hours and minutes and seconds we've talked and messaged and fucked behind Gerhard's back.

Still I have fantasies of breakfasts and lunches and whole days spent with David.

I pulled the tie tight, smoothing it over my chest and stomach.

"I like that shirt," he said, propping his head on his elbow. "But a brighter colour would be better."

I looked at the white fabric in the mirror. When am I going to stick by my decisions?

The kids envelope me, their hugs and kisses a pick—me—up after the three hundred kilometre trip. Three and four, one in each arm, I breathe in their newness and drop them into their seats at the table.

My wife sits at the table too, pert and pretty and blonde. She picks up the salad servers and deftly drops salad on the kids' plates. She is the perfect wife, unfussy and feminine.

I pull out my chair and wonder, what would I be doing if I were still in Sydney now, instead of home in Parkes three hundred kilometres away. Looking at the white of my plate, I can only see myself in a hotel room, with David. Would we be sitting in bed, watching television, or fucking?

But the nighttime fucking scenario doesn't fit. David would be home with Gerhard. And I would be … ?

I look at the three sitting around the table. Then see myself watching television in the hotel room, alone. And shudder.

Sometimes David and I connect, looking deep into each other's eyes as we fuck, rhythmed together. Sometimes it's in and out, come and go, see you next time.

I stepped into my sales manager's trousers, zipping the fly.

"Sorry I can't sneak in lunch with you," David said. "But work is maniacal at the moment."

I sat on the bed and pulled on my socks. And felt his eyes on me.

But this is madness. Three years is a good run. And how long is three years in affair years? A lifetime? A life sentence?

"It's a gorgeous view," David said, sitting up in bed and smiling. I looked out at the view: more hotel windows and a stuccoed wall. The beige art and design−free décor inside the room were more interesting.

But I'm tired of not being able to second−guess what he wants, I think, as the kids chatter about swimming in their new plastic pool.

"$30.00 at Go−Lo," my wife says. "Originally sixty." She reaches across the table for the salt. "Nearly had an aneurism blowing the thing up with my mouth!"

I watch her mouth as she forks lettuce into it and chews. *I'm really good at this*, she once told me as she slathered away on my cock, her hair tousled across her face.

Yeah, but I'm better, I almost said.

I tucked my shirt in then threaded the belt through the loops and breathed out. Then leaned over and kissed David long and soft on the lips, wanting to remember how they feel.

"See you," I said, taking in every millisecond of his face.

He nodded. I kissed his smile again, slipping my tongue inside. Then stood up and closed the door behind me.

My leather soles tolled a death knell as I crossed the hotel car park. I'll email that I can't meet him again, I thought, jaw firm, teeth grinding. Change my mobile number too.

I turned the key and put the car in reverse. Now I wouldn't have to make excuses for regular 600–kilometre round trips to Sydney either.

The lettuce on my plate reminds me that green is David's favourite colour. "Sorry, love," I say, pushing my plate away. "I'm not really hungry tonight."

And I remember that sandalwood is his favourite smell.

"Well, I made a gateau for dessert," she says, eyebrows raised in haughty disappointment.

"Is gateau your favourite, Dad?" the four year old asks.

"Yes," I answer. "I'll have more room by the time dessert comes around, I promise."

But what are promises?

I'll take half a Viagra tonight, I think. That will ease things for a week.

§

Waiting at the traffic lights, I looked at the flowers and gifts on the seat beside me, old tricks for my wife and kids.

My mobile 'phone rang and I snatched it up.

"Drive safely," David said. "Take a break halfway."

"Sure," I said. And wondered if this would be the last time we'd speak.

And then heard myself say, picturing myself vulnerable, legs in the air and his hard−on pressing inside me, "Can we do breakfast next time? I think I could swing an overnighter."

Dotting every 'i'

~

The network almost went into meltdown, we were so busy googling her name and experience.

"She seems eminently qualified," said Bernie my line manager, clicking on another link.

It was true: experience in publishing, business degrees from Harvard and some place in Switzerland.

And in person she was a knock−out: sleek blonde hair; long legs swathed in silk stockings or woollen trousers; a hint of perfume as she floated by with an expensive watch on her wrist.

"Just call me Amber," she said, rolling the 'r' − was her burr Swiss or American? We couldn't tell − looking each of us in the eye as she shook our hand. "I'm really looking forward to working with you."

"She had a weak handshake," I told Bernie when we were back at our desks. "Almost limp and gooey." I googled *weak handshake*.

Her presence in the building was immediate: a flash of blonde as she welcomed important writers into her office; calm but commanding footsteps on the plush carpet; her voice distant but everywhere.

Soon I felt her presence too: a journal article I had edited was returned from her desk with the words *cunt, pussy, cocksucker* and *fridge* crossed out.

"*Fridge*," I said. "What's so bad about *fridge*?"

"She's probably just establishing herself," Bernie said. "You know how these high–fliers are."

"Let me check with Amber," her red–haired assistant said, Amber's huge appointment diary tucked under her breasts.

"Yes," said her new assistant – a man with a crewcut – two days later. "Amber doesn't like the word *fridge*."

My fingers hesitant above the keyboard, I deleted *fridge* from the article.

The next week the same assistant stood at an editorial meeting and said, "Amber believes the division's publications are using too many adjectives. They're getting in the way of true meaning."

Silence around the table. I played with my blue pen, gave a large sigh and putting the fine white china cup to my parched lips, sipped refreshing green tea.

"Adjectives *can* be over–used," Bernie said. "We'll put a curb on them."

A week later Amber's new blonde assistant (sorry, the blonde who was newly assisting her) stood up at the meeting we had every week and said, "In the spirit of cost–cutting Amber has banned all apostrophes and commas."

"Thats not going to work" I said.

"Itll be cheaper and save time" the blonde said. "And to celebrate this decision Amber has invited you all into her office for drinks now that the workmen have refurbished and renovated it."

"Hot or cold drinks?" I said. The assistant looked at me.

I snuck in some adjectives to describe Ambers office: sleek and white with a view of the city we did not realise the building had. Mainly because a picture window had been knocked into the wall and a balcony added.

"I heard she got her business degree from the Mafia" one of the personal assistants said under her breath as we looked out at the view.

Amber watched as the blonde passed around glasses of champagne. Im sure Amber sipped the expensive stuff while the blonde handed around the cheap shit.

The next day a memo was sent around – adjectives are back it said as it was realised *not* using them actually meant using more words. But instead capital letters – except to start a sentence – were banned.

"But were a medical publisher for gods sake" i said (suddenly glad i was no longer forced to say *publisher of books to do with medicine*.) "Clear communication saves peoples lives."

Full stops at the end of sentences will also be phased out the memo said

"How do we do that?" i asked bernie "Use them only seventy–five percent of the time and then reduce them each week by a further twenty–five percent until we reach the target?"

"I dont know" whispered bernie as we stood at the urinal "Im looking for a new job"

Next week ambers new assistant – a chic korean girl fresh off the korea airlines stewardess programme – stood up and said "amber was asked to turn the profit margins of this division around and she has noticed you are not reducing your use of full stops quickly enough"

"But thats difficult" I said "We dont know the ruling on spaces between sentences"

"Amber has allowed an extra space between sentences to compensate" She smiled and flicked her black hair like she was dispensing relief to flood victims

"So does that include the space where the full stop would have been or does it mean there can now be three spaces between each sentence?"

"Can I get back to you on that?" she said

A memo came down later that day *As a space is less expensive than the ink of a full stop three spaces are allowed between each sentence But no more than three*

29

"Are they going to spend more money employing someone to count spaces now?" i asked bernie as a small group of us stood a block away from the office smoking the next day   I had given up smoking ten years earlier but smoking – amber was violently anti–smoking – was now an open act of rebellion

"And what about indentations" i said   "Is she going to ban those?"

"Why is it that you give a woman a bit of power and she turns into a man" said a new intern from the copying room "You can hear her balls rubbing on the carpet as she walks"

"Just keep your head low" bernie said to me   "She has her spies and she knows you made that remark about hot or cold drinks"

And then the monthly financials were published and costs were plummeting   Sales were plummeting too but costs were out plummeting sales so amber looked here to stay

I kept my head down

I ate my lunch in the staff room and made the usual mess on the table or sang jaunty ditties in the staff kitchen and had my excuses ready should amber discover my new fondness for indentations   I even asked ambers newest assistant – the korean girls twin sister – if she had a list of words we shouldnt use

"Let me get back to you on that" she said   "I cant breathe without it being cleared first"   And then covering her mouth she scurried away sobbing

"She was a nazi before she had her plastic surgery" said one of the managers in distribution

And what about the quality of care? other staff whispered – finally oh finally – as they slunk through corridors and listened out for the roar of ambers new mercedes–benz   As a medical publisher dont we have a responsibility to the medical profession and the general public?

Holed up in her office amber dispensed more edicts
No more using double leters

No more italics

No more punctuation of any kind including capital letters

cut out   third word   every sentence

staf thought   hit paydirt   she also   vwls

bt nfrtntly   mnthly fgrs   vn bttr

when wil someone do something i said that night on the phone to bernie refusing to speak without vowels *and* with al words included and in italics when i wanted

we should have a secret meting he said agreing to do the same

we can have it at my place I said only if she finds out youl have to say it was your idea

wr hvng   scrt mtng   tld vrybdy   wrk ts   tnght t plc

"This is my house," I said, standing up at the secret meeting. "And I'll spell and punctuate my sentences the way I see fit."

But no one volunteered to approach the company board.

That night, I lay in bed, eyes wide and head buzzing. I could picture myself marching into Amber's office and demanding the restoration of all punctuation, delivering ultimatums about employment conditions and editorial autonomy and damning her to the furnace of bad and ambitious bosses.

And then I turned and saw my wife, sleeping, beside me. And heard the soft breathing of our children in their bedrooms down the hallway.

And swallowed as I shut my eyes and attempted again to sleep.

And drove to work the next morning with the same overhanging dread.

mbr md   nncmnt t   wkly mtng

"I've changed my name to Ambré," Amber said, flouting her own rules as we looked on. "And anyone not putting in the accent will have their pay docked."

"And how much does she think that accent over the 'e' is going to cost?" I said at home in my soundproof bunker while flipping through the local job ads.

Then suddenly we found a notice on Ambers door: Back in three days.

And sensing a change, we slowly, timidly brought out our punctuation, double letters, *italics* and every third word from hiding.

"I've got a job with the government," Amber said at a meeting she called the morning of her return. "I'm heading the Red Tape Productivity Commission, starting today."

We raised our glasses of left−over cheap champagne and waved goodbye as she drove away in her Mercedes−Benz, towing her bowling alley behind.

Bernie thought she might have been given a fabulous separation package, but I think it was leave or get the sack. It was that accent over the 'e' that turned things around.

Never trust a weak handshake.

First Fish

~

"Just be yourself," said Jürgen, sitting on the edge of the bath eating *Stollen*.

"That has never worked for me," I said, putting my razor and shaving brush and shaving soap in my toiletries bag. Then taking everything out again and repacking it.

There were so many firsts that year: my first Christmas in Germany and my first Christmas in German; my first with Jürgen's family; their first *without* his soon−to−be ex−wife and their first with a *boyfriend* of his (i.e. me).

And it was Jürgen's first without his two sons too, because the soon−to−be−ex was feeling … motherly / vulnerable / spiteful. (Circle your choice.)

So everything was very … raw.

I had met Jürgen's family before, but three days and two nights with them under the same roof in Magdeburg?

Those present − Jürgen's parents, his sister and her partner, a cousin and a great aunt, and especially Omi (his grandmother) − all smiled and greeted me well in their quiet, reserved, northern German kind of way but double dotting my umlauts (ä ö ü) and saying *aaah* and not *ummm* (which sounds so native−English) when speaking German, was just exhausting.

And I felt so watched!

And perhaps I let my guard down – or kept it too far up – but sitting at the table on Christmas Eve next to Omi, I felt sure it was watching me too as it lounged – blue and dead, rubbery lips plump and pornographic – on the platter.

Surveilled, by a Christmas fish.

"*Karpfen blau* is very traditional," said Omi.

Traditional German or traditional north German or traditional to Sachsen–Anhalt or traditional to Magdeburg? Who knew which borders *Karpfen blau* respects in Germany.

"We *always* had *Karpfen blau* at Christmas when I was a girl," Omi said, spooning into the fish. "You must have some, David." And she plonked too much on my plate, piling the usual boiled potatoes with parsley next to it.

I scooped some up and as I closed my lips around the fork, saw everyone else had stopped eating.

They waited as I chewed under their gaze. The fish tasted vinegary and … muddy.

Picking bones from my mouth and tired of struggling with my poor German, I turned to Jürgen and asked, *auf Englisch*, "What's *Karpfen* in English?"

"Carp," he said.

My fork clanged on the plate as I dropped it. "Carp?! You eat carp for Christmas?"

"Well, only Omi," said Jürgen returning to German. "It's very traditional."

"You don't like it?" Omi asked.

I looked around the table. I had been the only one to join Omi in her remembrance of meals past.

"But it's a tradition," she said, her fork in the air.

I drank a glass of water, trying to drown the taste. And looked at the fish again, its blue sneer castigating me for my Anglo–weakness.

"We don't really eat carp in Australia," I said, picking up my wine glass and drinking that too.

I looked at the blank faces around the table and back to the carp's glassy stare. Was it daring me to continue?

"They're an official pest in Australia," I continued. "And if you catch one it's illegal to throw it back. They live on the bottom of the river in the mud and if you bring one with you to cook for dinner, people laugh at you or slam the door in your face."

Omi blinked, forking more fish into her mouth.

"This goose is delicious," said Jürgen. The family's murmurs were deafening.

My knife scraped on the plate as I pushed the carp aside.

When everyone had gone to bed and we were alone sipping *Glühwein* on the balcony, I finally breathed out.

Jürgen smiled. "You should have just eaten the *Karpfen*."

Monthly Coffee

~

Outside, we meet on the corner. She hugs me close, her perfume swamping me. I pull away, brushing hair from my face and make a mental note: suggest she buys different perfume.

Inside, she puts her faded red parka on the back of the chair, then – feet scraping on the polished concrete – pulls the chair out to sit at our usual table in the window. I look out at the cars and the people and the dogs on the wintry street.

"Are you okay, Mel?" she says, to my turned head.

I wish she wouldn't call me that.

"Yes," I say. "I'm fine." I look down at the clear varnish on my fingernails. I don't like to say much about my life, especially when her own is unfortunate.

She smiles her gappy, gold–toothed smile, hands jittery on the table. "How's your hubby going?"

"Robert's well," I say.

"And the kids are good?"

"The children are well, too."

She doesn't go the one step further though: how are my parents.

A waiter, darkly handsome and intense, hovers table–side.

"I'll have a cup of cino," she says, a standard order. "And my daughter will have the same."

"Yes, I'll have a cappuccino, please," I say, looking away. Though why I do this, I don't know: I never come here with anyone else.

My eyes wander around the room – at the production–line art covering the walls, junk shop mirrors, other patrons – but already I find it hard to concentrate. My mind is shopping, preparing dinner, on the 'phone, leading the rest of the life this woman gave me up to.

And for which, every month when we meet, I am always grateful.

I smile, and put a hand to my mouth, stifling a yawn.

"It's great to see you," she says again, her hands millimetres from mine on the table. "I'd really love it if we could see each other every week."

It always comes and I never know what to say!

"Well, I'm so busy with the children and we entertain so much with Robert's job. And Jonathan's rowing team is in the state finals."

Though what I really want to say is, this is all I can offer you, an hour once a month.

I look at her smoker's face. I could take her to a salon and have them ply her with crèmes and treatments … but she would tell them how we know each other.

Still, I would relish the contrast we make.

"I'm going to Germany again soon," I say, watching a laughing group of women as they pass the window and walk inside. "Leading another opera tour."

"It must be really exciting planning all these overseas trips," she says. Her fingers fidget, itching to light a cigarette.

But I don't smoke.

The waiter brings our coffee, and she smiles as he gives us our identical cups.

I keep saying 'she' but I can't call her 'Mum' though that's what she wants. She relinquished that name when she relinquished me as a baby. And calling her Pauline doesn't feel right either.

I look at the wrinkles around her colourless mouth and the bristles on her top lip. We look alike – without the moustache – but are nothing alike.

And she has no other children.

Funny, but I was the one whose questions turned to action, who filled out the paperwork and sought the first meeting!

But now, sitting here in the window as her talking swirls around me ...

I reach down and pick up my handbag, catch the waiter's eye and mouth I want the bill.

"I'll pay," I tell her, and smile. "Charity begins at home."

Lint

~

"I *cannot* believe you just did that!"

And Nathan looked at me, skewed, like a parent, dark eyes angry, jaw snapping under his wispy beard.

Paul gulped, choking back on the cafe latte he'd been drinking as he chuckled. And looked at me too, dimple chin glistening wet across the table.

I breathed in, the smell of coffee and hip talk and indignation filling my nostrils. And bent down in my chair to pick it up off the polished concrete floor. But Nathan grabbed my elbow and pulled me back, almost wrenching my arm from its socket.

"For Christ sake, don't embarrass me more!"

Suddenly the world stood still and every other patron in the café bored holes into me. The skin on my face prickled and flushed: I must have looked sunburned!

Paul put his glass down and his ring flashed – the ring I knew Nathan had given him – in the light. Oh, I thought I could roll with the whole gay ghetto this−is−my−ex−and−we−can−all−be−friends thing. But what did I know – I was wearing corduroy!

My hands sank into my lap as I sat back in the chair. I really wanted to say, *So, just what is it you see in me, Nathan?* But he had picked up his cup and was looking across it, at Paul.

"What did he say then?" Nathan continued, sipping.

"Oh well, you know. The usual," Paul said, and wiped his chin with the corner of his serviette, then looked at the stain before folding it and putting it in his pocket. "Just that it was nothing and he'd send the bill later."

Nathan laughed as he put his cup back on the saucer again. "He can be a bastard that way."

"Well, he was looking pretty peaky when he said it. I couldn't tell if he meant it or if it was just the gastro talking."

I took the menu from the centre of the table and eyes searching the page, pretended to study it. Did I want something to eat or did I just want to look busy? This kind of talk could go on for hours.

"Too much rich food will do that to you," Nathan said. "He needs to lighten up on the *beurre*."

I let the menu slip into my lap and looked across at Paul. I did not share his dimpled chin but we both had rich, thick sideburns creeping down our jawline. Nathan loved to run his fingers down mine, and then put his hand under my shirt – I still wore shirts then – and rub my stomach. "I adore your hairy stomach," he'd say. "It's so sexy." Paul must have had a hairy stomach too. That much facial hair usually travels.

"Are you still going to stay with Phyllis and Barry?" Paul asked, scratching his nose. Was that a secret signal? I had not yet met either Phyllis or Barry, but the visit was an annual one, something Nathan and Paul had done every summer when they were together.

"We haven't spoken about it," Nathan said. He sighed, glanced at me like I was a dummy in a storefront window, and scratched his chin. "I don't think Phyllis will like Mark."

Paul looked at me, a smile half playing on his lips – half saying exactly what, I couldn't tell – then turned back to Nathan. "No, you're probably right. I don't think she would like him."

Why wouldn't she like me? I wanted to ask, but at that moment the menu slipped out of my grasp to the floor and Nathan saw I had my hand inside my shirt again, fingernail digging, fingers rolling.

"No!" Nathan said. "Don't you *dare* pick more lint out of your navel and throw it on the floor!" He sat back in his chair, chin stuck out, eyes stony.

I bent down to pick up the menu. And looking up at the counter as the plastic slid further along the floor, saw the waitress – crisp white blouse, creamy complexion, light shining from her eyes – smile at me from behind the coffee machine.

"God loves you," she mouthed, though it was only Saturday.

And half in fear, half in relief, I half–smiled back.

Rainbow

~

"He walked in and slid the photograph across my desk," I said, putting the photo back into my handbag. "Which was really nice of Caspar, I thought."

Shona looked off to the left as we got off the bus, when she knew we had to walk right. A bitter wind blew up Turmstraße, and I was glad of our hats and scarves.

"Are you bored already, Shona?"

"No," she said. "Just a little incredulous that you let this Caspar guy – who you've never met before – into your apartment. Even if he does live in Moabit, too."

We waited until the pedestrian light turned green and crossed Turmstraße with everyone else.

Shona snorted. "Though knowing you, I guess it's not that strange."

We walked through the front door of *DM* and immediately slipped off our coats, scarves and hats. We both knew we would be there in the Drogeriemarkt – or health, home and beauty store – a while.

"I just thought it was really nice that he dropped it off," I said, bunching my coat over my arm. "He must really want me to work there."

"Or knows how desperate you are for money," Shona said, winding her scarf around her handbag.

"Every foreigner's desperate for money in Berlin."

"True," Shona said.

Like a heat–seeking missile, I turned into the aisle I wanted: so many brands, so many colours, so many prices and opportunities and instructions to follow. A smile spread across my face.

"But you're not even a lesbian, Katie," said Shona, eyebrows raised. "You don't even like men that much either."

"I know," I said, running my hand along the boxes of hair dyes. "He said he liked my aura."

"What he liked was your tits," Shona snorted. "You know, most women here wear a bra for warmth."

The hair dye packets were so bright and enticing, I wanted to take them all home, each offering a life–transforming dream, a beauty to chase after, a yearning for betterment at a price anyone could afford. I picked a copper highlights packet off the shelf and began reading the blurb.

"Well, I haven't got forever," Shona said, combing out her honeyed bob with her fingers. "I have to eat eventually, some century."

Then I picked an auburn gloss and a deep chestnut off the shelf too. "It's so hard deciding how I can personally interpret the photo he gave me."

Copper highlights? Auburn gloss? Deep chestnut? Copper highlights? Auburn gloss? Deep chestnut? I'd had every colour you could imagine at different stages in my life, but none had ever really suited me like the ash blonde I'd been now for eighteen months.

"I can't believe there's an official look you have to present when you're the Friday night door bitch at *The Bearded Clam*, for God's sake," Shona snapped. "Just choose something butch!"

I wedged the dyes under my arm and pulled the photo out of my handbag again. It was a black and white grainy bubblejet print.

"Where is this club, anyway?"

"In Schöneberg, Eisenacher Straße," I said. "Maybe he wants me to have the same *cut*." Not only am I blonde with shoulder–length hair but I'm also petite, and the woman in the photo had a dark crew cut with spikes at the crown and a hefty frame. "Maybe he gave me the wrong photo."

"Just dyke it up a bit," Shona said, looking through me. "Make a decision, buy the dye and let's get out of here."

But it would never be that simple. Shona sees things in black and white and I like to look for the rainbow in everything. Which is interesting, because our takes as English–language foreigners living in Berlin – and Germany – are very different: she likes its structure and innate orderliness, and I love the rent–a–hippies.

"I want to look sexy but not like I'm too available," I said. "Is that possible with a style like this?"

"What I really want to know is, why is a straight guy called Caspar opening a lesbian leather bar in Berlin anyway?" Shona asked. "Schöneberg must really be going to the dogs." She laughed – perhaps at her own joke? – then raised her eyes to the ceiling. She stomped off down the aisle and turned left.

"He said he's diversifying his assets," I said, louder, so she could hear me. "I think the lesbian leather market's the next big thing." I had no idea where she was going. Or really, what I was even saying.

I searched the photo for inspiration. I could go dark if I had to – I'd done it before – but really, that short short cut? My longish face and thin jaw – my brothers called me *Nosebag* – made finding a flattering hair–do a challenge.

Shona walked down the aisle towards me again, twirling something black. She stretched its rubbery form between her hands and let it twang back into shape.

"Hold still," she ordered, and stretching it wide, wide enough for me to think it might burst, she placed it over and around my head, snapping it snugly round my crown and ears.

"It's not leather, but rubber has a whole scene attached to it too ... so I hear."

"What is it?" I said.

"A bathing cap. You wear it when you go swimming. My grandmother used to wear one. Though hers always had flowers and other crap on it."

We scuttled around to the sunglasses so I could see what I looked like in a mirror. Predictably, a shop assistant – blue tunic and hair pulled back – scowled at us, so I took the cap off.

"He must be pretty definite about the hairstyle," I said. "Otherwise he wouldn't have delivered the picture to me."

Shona let out an exhausted sigh. "What are you going to do if he doesn't like you? You'll have ruined your hair for a job that went nowhere. I mean, you look less like a lesbian than I do."

"What does a lesbian look like?" I asked.

I glanced over at the shop assistant but she was not moving away. I wanted to see what the cap looked like on my head again, but didn't dare earn her Berlinerin glare.

"Oh for God's sake, I'll buy it," Shona said, ripping it from my grasp.

It was the one time there was no one queuing at the Kasse – unheard of in Berlin – and within seconds Shona had paid for the black rubber bathing cap and stuffed it in my handbag, rustling against the bubblejet print of the sample hair–do.

So, I had a rubber bathing cap I knew I could not wear, not even as trainee Friday night door bitch at a lesbian leather bar, and I still had no idea about what to do for the hair style.

"I really need to eat something," Shona said, as we stood a minute later on blustery Turmstraße, rugged up again in our winter woollens. "So I'll see you later."

She Euro–kissed me on each cheek and I dipped into my handbag.

"Then you should take this," I said, handing her the black bathing cap. "*You* should go for the job."

Shona stepped back, half–surprise on her face. But only half.

"And you should have this too," I said, giving her the photo. "You'd make a much better door bitch than me."

"Oh," Shona said. "Thanks." She stuffed the bathing cap and the photo in her handbag, convincingly, perhaps afraid I might change my mind. "I wasn't really ..." she trailed off, for once unsure what to say.

"You'd look good in that haircut too."

"Talk soon?" she said, half question, half statement, backing away.

"Sure," I replied.

She waved goodbye and hurried down Turmstraße.

I turned in the other direction and crossed Beusselstraße for the quick walk home. I knew Shona was planning to usurp me for the job anyway, I just wanted to avoid any unpleasantness. I don't have many friends in Berlin, and while Shona would probably call me a mad, hippy–dippy non–bra–wearing rainbow freak, her friendship was more important to me than a once–a–week job.

Sharp

Write

~

I pasted a sample paragraph of my writing on the website *Who do you write like?*

The response was immediate. I suddenly saw myself in long beard and flowing tunic, dispensing wisdom and loaves and fishes.

Switching off the computer, I caught my enigmatic smile on the blank screen.

My wife hurried past, holding an empty tray. "What're you smiling at?"

She disappeared, no time for an answer, door slamming.

I sat, considering this new enormity. I could found my own religion. Some man – prophet, seer, philosopher – develops a system of thinking and wham! they're building worship centres and theme parks and re–naming interstate highways after him.

Makes you think.

My wife hurried through again, tray stacked high with plates.

"I pasted a paragraph of my writing on the website *Who do you write like?* and it said I write like *The Bible.*"

She glanced as I followed her into the kitchen. She put the tray down, filled the coffee machine with tap water, spooned coffee into the two–cup filter, stamped it down vehemently, snapped the filter holder into place, flicked the on–switch, and stood, waiting for the first hiss.

She looked me in the face. "So I guess you'll be starting your own religion, then?"

"Why do you say that?"

"Because I did the same thing and it said I write like the Dalai Lama, so I thought we should move to Tibet. Coffee?"

Normally I'm allergic to bullshit but sometimes it can be a sneaky bitch.

Dishwasher

~

Last night aliens invaded our dishwasher. They activated the heating element. Everything inside that's plastic melted into the base of the dishwasher and we woke up coughing smoke.

"Fuck!" I said.

Brent rushed about, throwing all the windows open.

"Those aliens are fucking with our lives," I said later, filling the coffee machine.

Brent clasped his hands around the dishwasher. "I've found a website with many stories of the same thing happening with this model," he said. He pulled the dishwasher from under the benchtop and dragged it across the kitchen floor.

"Yeah," I said, stirring my coffee. "Those aliens are really fucked."

Brent pulled the dishwasher through the back door. "They're being recalled," he said. "They have a faulty timer switch." He pushed the dishwasher across the back porch.

"Exactly," I said, buttering an English muffin. "Aliens are getting inside and fucking with the timer switch."

Groaning, Brent lifted the dishwasher, hauling it to the bottom of the steps. Easing it down, he yelled, "Would you stop this alien bullshit, Tony! And stop saying *fuck* all the time!"

Munching on my English muffin, I watched Brent pull the dishwasher towards the driveway.

I went inside and turned on my computer.

DRAG THAT SHIT ONTO THE FUCKING STREET!!! I wrote on my blog. *ALIENS ARE BURNING DOWN OUR HOMES!*

Sitting at the computer, I could hear Brent's grunts as he pulled the dishwasher down the driveway.

And I wondered when to tell him about the alien in the hard drive.

der Morgenmuffel

~

She looked at me, morning–hazy, brows skewed but hopeful.

"Frau Kanzlerin," I said. "Be honest with them. Deutschland will love you for it and it could carry you beyond the 2013 election."

"*Ach so,*" she said. She patted her hair – typically, a mid–morning mess – and sipped her seventh coffee for the day. "*Dietmar, ich glaube, du hast recht.* Dietmar, you are right, I think."

I sat on the corner of her desk, and crossing my ankles and swinging my feet, looked past her hangdog wrinkles – caused by sleepless nights worrying about the Greece bail–out, immigration problems and Berlin's shitbag local economy – and smiled. Angela Merkel can be a sweetie when she wants to be.

I patted her on the hand. "Now, we can leak it through usual channels," I said. "Or do it officially. Or you can make a personal appearance on the new shopping channel premiering tomorrow."

"You choose, Dietmar," she said. "*Ich bin zu müde.* I am too tired."

Leider, the new shopping channel was scrambled – another victim of the Global Financial Crisis, just another wrinkle for the hardest working woman in German politics – so she said it off–

the−cuff quasi−officially in a *Bunte* interview: "*Ich bin wohl eher ein Morgenmuffel.*"

She hates mornings, she said. Next day, it made headlines in all the important newspapers, including *die Berliner Zeitung.* Look at her face and hair, they all said. Let her get up later and everything will get better.

Good call, though. Honesty is changing the course of history.

A smile is worth 1000 teeth

~

This set here I wear to fundraisers or the opera. They're smart but slightly sparkly. I love the contrast the pale pink gums make with the pearly teeth.

This second set have a great presence, they make a bold statement at the football or the races. Wearing them at equestrian events, I'm right at home in the stables.

This next set have low–slung gums: unfortunately, my lips curl behind them. They're too big for my mouth. I bought them hoping I'd grow into them, alas.

This set took a while to wear in, but they're great for holidays. The teeth fold in on the gums, they're easy to pack, very comfortable, so wash–and–wear and work well in extreme humidity.

This set here: 50% off, never worn them, too cheap and nasty.

Now these here are wonderful for weekends, they're not 'dress–to–impress' teeth, they just sit comfortably in my mouth, let me get on with gardening or preserving fruit or cleaning the carburretor or whatever.

And this set, they're my disco teeth. They look grey during the day so they're great for funerals. But they also flash in the dark so they're fun at parties.

These I'm wearing now were the first I bought, when my own were rotting stumps in my mouth. I was desperate for a social life but I couldn't go out because I was too embarrassed to smile. They're plain but serviceable, and changed my life. Which – believe me – is what good dentures can do for anybody.

Goose, and not turkey
or duck

~

"Admit it, you hate change," I said, shaking my newly−hennaed pageboy. "You're completely grey yet you still get the same perm every three months."

Bea scooped roast potatoes onto a serving plate. "Change is fine, Daphne, if it's for the better."

"Says the thirty year−old perm." I lifted the saucepan off the stove and poured orange sauce into a gravy boat.

"As always," Bea said. "Daphne's orange gruel."

I grabbed two mitts, opened the oven door and slid the goose out. Bea cleared space on the stone bench and I plopped the big bird on top, juices spitting.

"I'm not the one with three ex−husbands and another on the way," Bea added, covering the potatoes with a lid.

"At least when I get a new husband I trade up." I pierced the goose with two forks and, breathing in, lifted it onto the oval platter Bea placed beside it. Grabbing a carving knife, I sliced into the flesh.

"Everything looks up," Bea said, scraping carrots into a square dish. "When you start low."

I looked at her. And laughed, hard. Teary−eyed, I put the knife down. "That was a good one."

Bea smiled. "Yes, you can give me that one."

Mum walked in. "You two bickering like you do every year?"

"Yes, Mum," we said.

Mum opened a drawer, picked out a bottle opener and slammed the drawer shut. "Some things never change." And disappearing back into the party, she added, "That's what makes Christmas so special."

Kitchen Scrap

~

"It stopped me dead in my tracks," Valerie said, sitting in her darkened kitchen.

I nodded. Even in the gloom I could see the empty glass canisters, the shelves bereft of cookbooks, the apron hanging clean but dusty behind the door.

Her pudgy face, flour–coated and sugary and so life–nurturing in the past, had a different spark now, a searching look I'd seen as soon as she opened the door.

"So I gave away forty years of cookbooks. Gave away all the food in the cupboards and all my utensils."

"Even the old wooden rolling pins?"

"Yes," she said.

Oh, I had always loved watching those rolling pins work their pastry magic.

"What about meals?" I asked.

"My daughters both have me over once a week," she said. "Sometimes I go out for dinner. Sometimes I don't." She smiled thinly.

I wiped the dust from the island cupboard where we were sitting – once the workspace for so many handsome feasts – and clasping my hands in front of me, considered what to say.

"You could have had the gas reconnected," I said. "Having your gas accidentally cut off isn't a sign from God that you should stop cooking."

Valerie laughed. "No, it didn't seem so at first."

She hugged her elbows and looked at me.

"I gave my neighbour my kettle," she said. "So if you want coffee, you'll have to go next door."

The Deepest Cut

~

Smoke is pouring outta my ears! (And outta my mouth and nostrils, but that's normal.)

The Fast–o–matic Supermart has changed their coupons. Now you can't swap them for plastic surgery. So all those tubes of New Orleans–style Cottil–i–Lard dog sausage were bought for nothing.

And New Orleans–style Cottil–i–Lard flavour is not my favourite.

"Next election is gonna be real interesting," I said, wearing army fatigues as I stood in the check–out line swapping coupons for rubber sheeting.

"Why's that, Maureen?" said LaVern, patting her hair.

"The little people have had enough and there's gonna be a revolution."

"All 'cos you can't get discount face smoothing anymore?"

Where that LaVern leaves her brain, I got no idea.

"It's more than just my face, LaVern," I said, handing her the coupons. "Even my thighs have crow's feet."

"It's a free country," she said, popping the coupons in the cash drawer and pushing the rubber sheeting towards me. "No one ever made you smoke."

"If the government wants us to smoke so they can take our taxes, they should give us free plastic surgery so we can get rid of our smokers' wrinkles."

LaVern leaned over the conveyor belt and said under her breath, "Sounds like socialism, Maureen."

Ever since LaVern went to that community college last summer she uses these big words.

"Have fun looking *socialism* up in the dictionary," LaVern said, as I stuffed the rubber sheeting in my titanium—dipped carry—all.

I love this country but it's going to the dogs.

Verboten

~

Casey is a big woman. I was reminded of this at the airport, my hug unable to circumnavigate her.

So Berlin summer 2009 proved challenging. Because fat people were banned from taking the S—Bahn.

Dicke Leute verboten, the black and yellow signs read. *Fat People forbidden*.

Scales were installed on station platforms. Those who were overweight were turned away.

These were extenuating circumstances. S—Bahn authorities had not kept up regular maintenance. A derailment revealed faults with thousands of carriages. Some train lines went from running every three minutes to every twenty. Others were cancelled indefinitely.

Commuters were also asked to leave bikes and pushers home, saving space on the too—infrequent services. And Berlin newspapers published *Die offizielle S—Bahn Diät*. It included – as exercise – *not* taking the S—Bahn, and eating low—fat würstchen.

Still, one day, we shoehorned Casey onto the S—Bahn. Other train—goers glared. And her voice – brash, nasal, American – echoed throughout the carriage: "God, it's so crowded in here!"

"Yes," said an older Berlinerin, her English accented. "And you are taking all the oxygen."

The comment was fair. Casey is a heavy breather.

We soon realised the six-station trip to Alexanderplatz was impossible, and got off at Bellevue. We thought we would work on our tans in Tiergarten. But we were stopped at the entrance to the park by a guard, forbidding grimace barring our way.

Casey was too fat for the park, he said. There is an official allowance of sun per person, and Casey had exceeded the limit.

Bus

~

Packing it was like playing tetris. One thing on top of another, building layers, my multi-coloured life seen through the large windows of a 35-seater bus.

"It's not working," Veronica said. "There's no way we'll make the emergency evacuation queue in time, Dad."

I studied her fifteen-year old face, seeing nothing similar between us. She looks just like her mother, I thought, whoever the anonymous egg donor was.

"That's very obsessive compulsive gay," she added. "You can't take a chandelier on an emergency dash across a nuclear desert."

Ah, but her eloquence! *That* she gets from me.

The back door slammed as Marvin stepped outside.

"Dad wants to pack a chandelier in the event of a nuclear attack," Veronica said. "It's ridiculous."

"Could it be used for something besides providing an elegant setting for dining?" Marvin asked, stroking his beard. "Multi-purpose objects should be given a chance to prove their manifold uses."

Veronica threw her hands in the air. "Neither of you are taking this seriously," she said. "You think it's a joke."

She walked away and stood against the fence post, arms folded, scowling. My heart thumped in my chest. Times like this I truly loved her, her grumpy teenage face a life force.

I walked over and put my arms around her. "What do you want me to take out?" I said softly.

She leaned into my shoulder. "Those caftans for a start," she said. "Except the white one. That could work well at a post–apocalyptic toga party."

Always Vera

~

"How much more of my money are you spending, Phil?"

My mother watches through thick glasses, chin wispy in the sunlight, as I put her old—fashioned bank book back in her bedside drawer.

"The price of everything's gone up," I say. "But I don't have to buy you chocolate if it's costing too much."

She says nothing and bends her head again, gnarled hands slowly breaking a family—sized chocolate block into pieces.

I brush chocolate crumbs off the white sheet before they melt and smear, then thump her pillows into submission and replace them behind her back.

"No one listens to me here," my mother says, leaning back on the pillows. "You're never here long enough, and none of the nurses or carers or cleaners or cooks can be bothered." She pops two chocolate pieces in her mouth. "Thank God for Vera. *She* always listens."

Only friends four weeks and it's always Vera now.

I put my hand to my mouth, stifling a yawn.

"It's good that you have a new friend," I say. Though I want to say, *Why don't you get Vera to do your personal shopping and pay your bills and keep you connected with the outside world?*

"Vera brought me a cake last week. 'Course I couldn't eat it – too rich." She pushes two more pieces in her mouth, her teeth gooey brown. "If you stay, you can meet her later. She's bringing me some magazines."

I open my mouth to answer, but stop. And watch as she munches more chocolate.

We meet in the nursing home car park, out of sight of my mother's window. Vera looks exactly like the photo she sent responding to my ad: piggy eyes, doughy face, wiry salt–and–pepper hair. And chin stubbly in the sunlight.

"It's nice to see you again, Vera," I say.

"Yes," she says. "Where's my money?" She laughs her smoker's rasp.

I only half–smile, and place $100 of my mother's money in her open hand. I notice the magazines she's brought are dog–eared. The print will probably be too small too.

"That's $25.00 for one visit a week," I remind her.

"I baked her a cake so I'll need to get my money back for the ingredients too," she adds.

I slap another $20 in her palm. "I'll see you in four weeks' time. Make sure she doesn't find out."

Vera reaches into her blouse and stashes the money in her stupendous bra. "Mum's the word."

First

~

"I grew tired of waiting," she said.

White−knuckled, she gripped the clacking needles so ferociously she could have knitted the booties in gale force winds and they still would have turned out ankle−stranglers.

"You were always too busy building your train set."

She smoothed her new pink−and−white−vertically−striped way−too−roomy smock over her stomach. Then counting stitches under her breath, she cast off.

She was right. Building the train took over a year. I gutted the second bedroom, turning the bay window into storage for spare rolling stock. Then I built a mezzanine for a replica of the Berlin U−Bahn, the grungy flower kiosks and bored commuters painstakingly realistic.

Now the thought of pulling it all down to make room for a baby zapped my strength.

"I can't believe you went ahead and got pregnant without me," I said.

"Well, you have a whole six months to get used to the idea," she answered, knotting baby−blue yarn on the end of the row. She resumed her clacking, loudly. My lack of energy was fuelling hers.

"Don't worry," she added. "You'll get a crack at the next one."

"I could have downed tools for – what, two minutes? – to impregnate you myself."

She threw her knitting in her lap. "Stop it, Brian! Just be thankful it'll have red hair like you and no one will notice."

That was true too. My identical twin brother had stepped into the breach and defended the family honour. Born five minutes before me he was still coming first.

Arrivals

~

The key scratched in the lock and his travel bag skidded across the floorboards as he threw it inside.

Floating candles glowed on tables.

'His' and 'His' towels hung in the bathroom.

The poppers, the Viagra, the chorizo – all had been ordered and all had arrived.

I hugged his broad shoulders, kissed him long on the lips, and then I saw it – a tattoo.

"Where did you get this?" I asked, fingertips tracing the *666* on his forehead, red and bumpy.

"What?" he said.

I looked into his eyes.

"Oh, that," he said, hand closing his fringe over the new scar. "It's a lot less offensive when I stand on my head."

He smiled, walked down the hallway, and closed the toilet door behind him.

My knuckles rapped softly against the wood.

"Who is it?" he said.

"I think we need to talk, Nathan. What's happened?"

He opened the door a crack, fully dressed. "Oh, you know," he sighed. "My endless search for meaning. Sometimes things can take a bit of a wrong turn."

I reached for his forehead through the doorway but he flinched.

"No," he said.

I stood beside the closed door for a full five minutes. Once, perhaps, I heard muffled sobs.

"Can I get you anything?" I asked.

"Some chorizo would be nice," came his voice from the other side. "You can leave it on a plate by the door."

Berniece

~

Justin cradled her head in his hands as she breathed her last. Berniece had been a good dog. But she was also twenty years old – blind, bald, bedridden, deaf, diabetic, and doubly–incontinent. We should have had her put down years before but Justin couldn't bear the thought.

We buried her in the back garden with full honours. Then I snuck off to make the call from my mobile in the car.

"I offer a professional service, Mr Smith," the hitwoman said over the 'phone. "I charge a cancellation fee."

"But Berniece died of natural causes," I said.

"I'm not an amateur." Her voice was measured and menacing. "You told me your home had smelled of dog excrement for five years. And I offered you relief from that. I expect 50% of the agreed fee. In cash."

I dropped the envelope at the designated spot and parked up the street.

Leisure–suited at a snail's pace, she came walking three ancient, droopy dogs. Dipping behind the bush, she took the envelope, put it in her pocket, and walked on.

I got out of my car as she drew nearer. She glanced at me from behind huge sunglasses, red lipstick bleeding into the wrinkles around her mouth. Serious grey hair, svelte and bobbed, framed her face.

"Nice dogs," I said, knowing they were probably dribbly and demented.

"Yes, they're my life," she said.

I watched her turn the corner. And wondered how much blood money was keeping those dogs alive.

Body to Go

~

I'm squatting naked over the hand mirror, feet cold on the terrazzo floor, looking at my winking arsehole. It reminds me of her face: eyes sloe, nose tiffed, lips harrumphing. And the badge bobbing above her right breast: '*Tiahna – your friendly trainee*'.

I glop the paintbrush in the crab lotion and slather it on my hole, perineum, under my balls. I favour broad strokes – no pointless pointillism – but stab the cracks and folds precisely. The crab lotion tingles and burns, stinging all senses.

And I have my entire body to go! Arms, chest, stomach, underarms, back, pubic hair, legs, feet, toes.

Yes, I am *that* hairy. Yes, the crabs have taken over.

EARLIER

Tiahna – factory–fresh, rust–free, go–go–figured circa nineteen year–old Norwood Chemist junior – inched the *Benzemul Application* bottle from the top shelf.

"Do you sell paintbrushes too?" I asked.

She handed the bottle to me, nostrils glaring.

My head steamed. "I might be forty–nine but I can still get crabs!" I said. "Which you get from *fucking*."

75

Distaste churned in her face.

"I'm *infested* with pubic lice," I spat. "I need a lot of paintbrushes to apply this stuff. Although a dipping vat would be better, but I bet you don't sell vats either."

Tiahna shook her head, scanning and bagging the *Benzemul* bottle.

LATER

I unfold to a stand, forty–nine year–old knees cracking. Swapping to a broader brush, I slather my chest. Then stop.

A paint roller would work so much better. And I'm scratching to see Tiahna again.

Big Dipper

~

"How do you expect to find a husband, Leona, if you have such high standards?"

"I know, Mum," I said. "And normally I adore Americans."

My counsellor insists I call her *Mum*. At first I thought it was strange, but I see her point: she's the right age, my own mother is extremely deficient in the role and we don't look unalike. Especially after she bleached her hair, lost weight and started dressing like me.

I pushed my sunglasses on top of my head – she says wearing sunglasses inside makes me look like I'm hiding something, though with my pink eyes, usually it's just to keep the harsh light out – and examined the cuticles the Vietnamese nail girl had just finished.

"You're not in Saigon anymore, Mai Bi'ch," I said, craning to read her name badge. "They'll need to be much better than that if you want to stay in this country."

Mai Bi'ch looked at me, looked at the nails, and pushed my fingers back into the bowl of nail softener.

"I said, *I love chips with tomato sauce*, and he said, *You mean French fries with ketchup?* Now, where do you go from there?"

Mai Bi'ch readjusted the facemask over her nose and mouth, pulled my hand from the goo and attacked my cuticles with an orange stick.

"Ow!" I said, though it didn't really hurt. And turning to Mum I added, "*And* he double−dipped his chips in the sauce."

"Oh," said Mum. "I see what you mean."

Arms Width

~

She flicked the curtain open. The badge above her left breast said *Valerie*.

Standing in the changing cubicle, dressed only in bra and trousers, I hugged the blouse I'd just taken off to my chest.

"Need another size, love?"

The hair on my neck stood on end. *Love*?

"That mauve goes nicely with your hair."

I caught sight of my salt–and–pepper hair in the mirror. Her saleswoman skills were working overtime.

She sank against the cubicle wall and – white–blouse–and–black–skirt bulging over her body – blocked the view. Kiss curls stuck to her cheeks, her dyed–orange hair and thick makeup unkind in the artificial light.

"But you've got all the same style there, love," she said, waving her false nails at the blouses hanging on hooks.

I put a coathanger through the neck of the mauve blouse I had just taken off and hung it up.

"You've got your blue, your pink, your red, your avocado, your cream and that mauve."

Trying them all on to make sure they fitted, I took the blue blouse off its hanger, slipped it over my head and gingerly pushing my arms through the armholes, pulled it over my hips.

But it was like all the others: baggy at the waist, hanging at the bust, and tight around my arms.

"Ooh, they are big, aren't they?" she said. And grabbing my upper arms, she squeezed them.

Pendulous and flabby, fleshy drapes hanging between my armpits and elbows, my upper arms are the bane of my life when buying clothes. I'd promised myself that when I turned forty, I would have them reduced. Filleted and refashioned. And now, at almost sixty, they were flabbier than ever, thwacky windsocks under her touch.

I snatched my arms away.

"No need to be scared, love." And she turned and closed the curtain.

I felt a hook on my neck as I backed against the wall. My mouth dropped as she reached into her bra.

"Ever thought of doing porn?" she said, cigarette breath hot on my face. "'Cos your arms would go a treat in the fetish world." And she handed me a business card.

I looked at it.

"You'd make good money," she smiled. "And you'd be a big star in Japan."

She pointed to the card. *Summer Bangs – Adult Entertainment Talent Scout.*

I looked in her eyes. They were small and pale blue and hard to find behind her mascara and bags.

"If I was going to do anything," I said. "I'd have my arms reduced."

She laughed. "Ooh, there's no longevity in porn, love. Make your money while you can, then get your arms done with your earnings. It's win – win for everyone."

She smiled. And stood, waiting.

I stood, waiting.

But she stood longer.

"I'd have to think about it," I said.

She reached into her bra again and took out another card: *Nancy Smith – Registered Nurse.* "'Cos I know a wonderful plastic surgeon. And afterwards, he could do a lovely job on your arms."

Love

~

"I've met someone," Trent beams down the 'phone.

Thank God, I think. The drought has broken.

"You must meet him."

Standing on the corner, I wonder if Trent's new boyfriend will look like any of the exes: tall and muscled, like Rodrigo, Manny and Bruce? Petite and muscled, like Kim, Jackie and Ba? Or hairy and muscled, like Spike, Max and Bruce (doing double duty ten years and a new body later)?

"Hi, stranger." Trent's arms enclose me. A bursting warmth shines through his eyes.

"This guy's worked wonders," I say.

"I'm like a new man," Trent trills. Then holds up his hand, as if pledging allegiance. "Wait: I *am* a new man!"

"Come in," he says, leading me through a side door. And into a church. Which I'd noticed while waiting but thought was just a meeting point.

Trent stops before a statue of a buff Jesus. "Meet the new man in my life."

Trent's had many phases: Madonna, Bette, leather, water sports, rollerblading, haiku, chicken queen, rice queen, muscle queen, daddy. But religion? This is *new*.

But there's no denying Trent looks a different – certainly happier – person.

"How serious is this?" I say.

He lays his hands on my arm. "Come with me to my prayer meeting tonight."

I look for a chink, to find the Trent I've always known.

"I can't," I say. "I have a date with the devil."

"Oh," he says. But I see the familiar spark in his eyes. "Tell him I said hello."

Shiny

A Free Rinse

~

"What are you doing?" Daniel said. It was New Year's Day. And eyes unfocussed, mouth tinder dry and unable to string three words together, I was filling a bucket with water.

The answer lay outside in the next−door neighbour's front yard, too many decibels too loud for 9.00am, creating newly−mown strips in the lawn.

"That fucker's gonna wake the kids," I said, completely sober.

Daniel knew not to stand in my way. He didn't say *Think about what you're doing*, or *What about neighbourhood relations?* or even *Do you want any help?* He just held the back gate open as in my brief, new pink−and−white bathers (swimsuit or trunks or togs or swimmers to others), bucket of water slapping at my side, I charged down the driveway.

The fucker had woken me up, and I did not want him waking up Daniel's grandchildren (two and three years old) either.

And I knew the garden hose wouldn't reach.

I sped along the footpath in the sun, head fuzzy but anger mounting as, his eyes downward, the next door neighbour − grey and tall and in his own world − marched up and down the lawn, pushing that fucking lawnmower.

I stepped towards the waist–high fence. Where to throw it? At him, in his blue polo shirt with the iced coffee logo above the left breast and fawn cotton trousers? Or at the black metal–and–plastic lawnmower?

Which would have greater impact?

And which would have greater legal repercussions?

I grabbed the bucket lip with my spare hand, my head still woolly and my mouth sleepy–dry – he still had not seen me – and lifting it up, hurled the water at him.

This was the culmination of twelve years of neighbourly aggro. Of thoughtless lawn–mowing on early weekend mornings. Of snapping over–hanging apricot tree branches at the fence line (when he could have kept the apricots); of needless whines about water seepage and letters left in our letterbox about winter gutters and getting his cement wet (and threatening to tell … someone); of watching him during a lightning storm (yes!) brushing other neighbour's leaves from his roof (not the gutters, the roof!); of his obsessive house–pride because he had little to do beyond piss everyone else off with his petty demands and stupid behaviour. We were his only neighbours who had not raised our fence.

And now, he was stamping his mean spirit on the new year before anyone else had the chance to draw breath, lassoing the new decade with his spite and telling the world it was his to do with as he pleased.

So, the gesture was small, but my meaning was epic.

The empty bucket swung at my side as he gasped and stepped back. Water drenched his chest and trousers and soaked the lawnmower, though still it roared.

"Turn the fucking thing off!" I yelled above the noise. "It's fucking New Year's morning!"

He replied – with what I don't know and cared about even less – and so, bald–headed and hairy–chested, I spat the words out again. "It's too early in the morning! Turn the fucking thing OFF or I'll do it again!"

His wife – smoke–wrinkled and flossy–haired, her mouth skewed in anger – stepped onto their front porch.

"Turn the fucking thing off!" I yelled at her too.

The lawnmower still drowned out all noise, but I kept on.

"You're a pensioner. You can mow your lawn any time!"

And I waved the bucket at them and set my jaw and glowered.

But I had made my point, and shaking in my thongs (flip–flops or jandals to others), I turned and walked back up the driveway, lawnmower still choking the atmosphere.

Closing the front door behind me, Daniel half–smiled. "They'll probably call the cops."

"What for?" I said. "Assault with a wet weapon? Drowning personal property?"

And they did.

Snack

~

They were the weirdest family in the neighbourhood: father tall and rake thin, hardly ever seen except driving to and from his job at the nearby hardware shop (the one with the fundamentalist Christian slogans in the windows); son and eldest daughter of similar builds and clearly two bricks short of a load. And the squat mother was apparently – so we learned later – extremely intelligent, loved classical music and even went to church (Anglican, even more surprising) but to look at her lumping home from the bus stop, breasts bobbing and hips heaving with each step, you'd never have known she was a MENSA candidate. And she gave her looks to their youngest, Kerryn.

Kerryn's name didn't help either, in a suburb filled with Kylies and Kerrys and Karens. She was older than we were (me, my two sisters and three other kids from two other houses in the street) and outclassed us in the puberty stakes, boisterous cleavage unrivalled at the primary school we all attended. She probably should have been in high school, even then.

Kerryn's hands were damp to the touch, and her eyes would dart about her freckled face and the schoolyard and the neighbourhood and she would clutch her swishing skirts in an adult way – half–knowing, half–nervous, all clumsy. Her voice was small, barely audible at times, her hair thin and mousy and often oily, though sometimes fluffy and clean, perhaps just after she'd washed it. She snuffled too and at times smelled of stale urine and perspiration, so playing dress–ups when we were all together was very hit–and–miss. Was it too rude even for kids to suggest dry–cleaning the can–can skirt we all fought over (and wore inside out, blue and green frills showing – I was eldest and bossiest so wore it often) after Kerryn grabbed it, slipped it over her head and it snuggled about her waist? Regardless, we all avoided wearing it the next week.

One day we found an old crust of bread, thick and stale and curled at the edges, too burned for breakfast and probably tossed on a front lawn or footpath for unfussy birds, or a refugee from a neighbour's bin on rubbish day. (Bits of old bread seemed to settle about the street in ways then that are unfamiliar now.)

But on a bright spring day, we smeared greeny–brown dog shit, pungent and crunchy, across its dry surface with a thick twig, fingers crooked to avoid contact. (Dog shit seemed more plentiful then too.)

"Here Kerryn, would you like some bread with peanut butter?" we said. We thought politeness would mask the smell.

But we could barely contain ourselves, smirks bubbling across our faces, the greeny–brown smear offered like a sacrifice.

"It's really delicious," we said. "Mmmm."

(How did we serve it? On a stray paper plate, also leftover from someone's rubbish? A piece of newspaper? An old bit of wood? Actually, I think we braced ourselves and served it *au naturel*. Or rather, I did, the only one brave enough to touch the crust, gingerly cupped in my hand, dog shit authentically almost to the edges.)

Kerryn shocked us by backing away, nose wrinkled in horror. And maybe shocked it was us doing the offering.

"Mum gave us some before," we added. "So we're not hungry now."

The closer the open dog shit sandwich came the further Kerryn pulled away. We tried not to smile, not wanting our barely controlled snickers to give us away. But she turned on her heels and arms in full sail, bottom bouncing, ran up the street and around the corner and home.

Really, the joke was on us. She was smarter than we'd thought.

Perhaps it was another incident – sitting on the neighbours' table tennis table, Kerryn slid off to leave an expanding pool – that prompted our generosity.

"It's lemonade," Kerryn had said. "I spilt it." And she ran home then at full sail too, wet bottom bouncing up the street and around the corner. She might have been twelve at the time, and me ten.

Kerryn saved us from ourselves really. Would you be reading this had she eaten it?

And thinking back to the table tennis table and what I have come to know now, I wonder if she wasn't abused.

I Swear

~

I heard people, when I was living in Germany, swearing in English, when they would never swear *auf Deutsch*.

I once heard a woman when I was living in Hamburg in 2008, in her 50's or perhaps early 60's, say "Shit!" as she jumped on a train. Then listening to her conversation soon after, it became quite clear the few words in English she knew and used were all swear words.

Often the first words we learn in new languages are swear words. Sometimes this is amusing. Sometimes it's not.

Swearing and cursing (are they the same?) hold different places in different languages. It is definitely worse to swear in German, or rather, in German culture, than it is in English-language cultures, in general.

Certainly it's worse to swear in Germany than it is in Australia.

I swear quite a lot, at times, and often don't even know I'm doing it. I would talk with Australian friends in Germany and we would be having a normal conversation, and German friends would look at us askance. The swearing peppering our conversation was just normal for us. Others thought we were angry. Or uncouth. Or maybe both.

In some languages swearing is always used when angry. In Australia, and perhaps in other English language cultures, this is not always the case. It would not be that unusual for me to say to an Australian friend – in Australia or in Germany – *Can you pass me that shit, please?* Which actually means, *Can you pass me that thing?*

Hence the askance looks.

I actually love using swear words in their proper context. *Shit* when you are talking about defecating; *cock* when you talk about penises; *fuck* when you talk about sex. (Half the Americans have stopped reading by now.) In these examples, you are actually using these words correctly.

(I once went on radio – admittedly community radio, a gay and lesbian cultural show – when I worked in the HIV / AIDS sector in Australia, and without even realising it, talked about *fucking* while on air. I used it to mean penetrative anal sex, which is the term used in the sector, in brochures, in leaflets, in campaign materials, in advertising, in fact, whenever HIV / AIDS prevention is mentioned. The presenter went white and off–air seconds later, told me I had said *fucking* on–air. My first thought was "And? ..." ... and then I realised. And then I thought, well, too fucking bad, if you want to get all prissy about it, good luck to you! No one complained about it later. And the world kept turning.)

And bilingual Germans will quickly tell you that yes, it *is* worse to swear in German than in English. Saying *Scheißekopf* is worse than saying *Shithead.* Formal politeness is revered in Germany. This stiffness often gets me down. It means nothing – or little – and seems to be just another shield for Germans to hide behind. It's not really about how others regard you, but instead about not allowing them to get to know you.

What I would really love to do is to take a poll in Germany. Which is worse: *Du bist eine alte Fotze?* Or, *Sie sind eine alte Fotze?*

Du bist is the familiar form of *you are.*

Sie sind is the polite form of *you are.*

So, if you were talking to an old woman on the street you did not know, you would normally say, *Sie sind.*

And just so you know, *eine alte Fotze* means *an old cunt.*

So which is worse, saying *You are an old cunt* using the familiar 'you' (*du*) or saying *You are an old cunt* using the polite 'you' (*Sie*)? Discuss.

(I think you can argue either way.)

Calling someone an old cunt in Australia is offensive too – actually, you can't say much worse – BUT the word *cunt* can be used in an affectionate way. "Ah, she can be a bit of a cunt, but she's okay." It's like saying, "He's an old bastard, but I love him anyway."

Of course, the circles in which you can say this – and in which it's taken the right way – are limited. But it is possible.

I once spent thirty minutes of an English lesson teaching the various meanings of the word 'fuck'. I was teaching Business English to a small work group in Berlin in 2009 – actually, I loathe teaching Business English, as usually it's just made up on the spot, and so often taught by others who have absolutely no experience in the world beyond studying and teaching – and the youngest and hippest of the group of six men said, when talking about playing hockey, "That was before I fucked up my knee."

I said, "You used the word *fucked.*"

The room went silent as the six men looked at me, wondering where I was going with this.

"*Fuck* is a very versatile word, and we use it all the time in English, so let's talk about how it's used," I said.

There may have been some blanched looks, there may have been some glottal gulps, but we talked about it anyway.

And its uses are varied and deep:

★ as a verb, and especially as a phrasal verb – I am fucking, I am being fucked, Fuck me!, I've just been fucked, we fucked on the bed, I fucked it up, you fucked it up, I'm being fucked over, he's fucking me over, I'm fucked off, I am so fucked up, Fuck off!

* as a noun – I need a fuck, that fuck was great, he's a great fuck, he's a real fucker!

* as an adjective – I'm a fucking arsehole, you're a fucking arsehole, hand me that fucking thing, it's a fucking nightmare, you're a fucking mess, I don't need that fucking shit, I'm fucked, that's fucked, we're all fucked, it's just fucked, we're all going to hell in a fucking handbasket!

'To fuck' *auf Deutsch* is *ficken*. And German–language online profiles will sometimes have the words *Fick mich!* (*Fuck me!*) on them, but interestingly, if the person with the profile speaks and writes English – which many, many do – they will usually use *fuck* and not *ficken*. There's something open and gaping and sexy about the 'u' sound in *fuck* that is absent in *ficken*. 'U' sounds more like an orifice.

So, when I am swearing my head off and not even knowing I am doing so, I feel most at home in Australia. And while it is fun to shock Germans with my swearing proficiency, *auf Deutsch und auf Englisch* – okay, I rarely say *cunt*, because (1) it really is offensive and (2) I've never actually been there – it is nice to be not so soundly, roundly judged for the disgusting words coming out of your mouth.

Jacqueline Bisset and Me

~

Years ago I read an article on the English actress Jacqueline Bisset – you know, English–born, speaks fluent French, works in America and France and oh, lots of places, was once voted the most beautiful woman working in cinema – and I have never forgotten how in the article she spoke about being a different person when she speaks French.

You can see it on the screen.

Acting in English, she is often formal and stiff and even remote. No one could ever accuse her of being an old ham. And to be honest, I have never found her that appealing when she acts in English: she can act, she's just not very warm.

But watch her acting in French – in Francois Truffaut's *Day for Night* (1973), or more correctly *La nuit américaine*, even when it's dubbed into English, or more amazingly Claude Chabrol's *La Cérémonie* (1995) – and she's a completely different person, warm and fluid and open and even, given that she is supposed to be *acting*, happy. I was blown away watching Bisset in *La Cérémonie*. This is the woman she should always have been! Where had she been hiding?

Perhaps Bisset was helped by having Isabelle Huppert, surely one of the world's most–celebrated non–emoters, playing one of the leads in *La Cérémonie*. But that's another story.

(I once asked a Polish friend, whom I thought was actually American when we first met in Berlin, if she was a different person in English. And she said simply, "Yes.")

When I am back living / staying / killing time / enjoying southern summer in Australia, and not living in Berlin, I miss speaking German (*oder Deutsch*). I compensate for this by talking about speaking German and German words and living in Germany (particularly Berlin) and the German influence on English, through the Angles and the Saxons, and perhaps the Jutes too, though the Jutes always seem to be forgotten. I do this endlessly, and I do this mostly when I am teaching English. So many English words derive from Old German, so the practice is endless. And connecting for me. And perhaps a shade dull for my students … though still I persist.

Actually speaking German in Germany – *Schuldigung, aber mein Deutsch ist bisschen* – can be a trial. It makes me nervous and sometimes irritable, but boy it's wonderful – *fast unglaublich* – when Germans respond in German and we converse – actually have a conversation – without any English. It makes me feel almost international.

Speak quickly, using words or phrases you know are correct and have practiced often, and with a good accent, and native–speakers may even think you are a native speaker too. Well, *vielleicht.*

I know when speaking, I am generally quieter, meeker, softer, more careful *auf Deutsch.* Though I think my fluency accounts for this. If I had better German, then I would be more myself when speaking it.

Mostly though, when speaking German, I love getting my tongue around the words, attempting to sound as authentic as possible. It's a performance, I know this, and I must confess that I find embarrassing those non–native German speakers (usually native English speakers) who seem to make no attempt at speaking Deutsch with an even faintly convincing accent. *Listen to how you sound!* I want to say. I don't, of course, for fear that I, in fact, sound just as bad.

But it's wonderfully affirming to be told you have a good accent in another language, and I have been lucky to have been praised, on a few occasions, for my good German accent, and this by native German speakers. I have taken these as rare compliments!

One friend, an English–into–German translator and subtitler, once said I did not have an accent at all when I spoke German. This seemed incredible to me. I even said to her, "But I must have an accent — surely an Australian accent — when I speak Deutsch." She said again I didn't. Where lies the truth?

German *is* a great language for sounding angry, though. The guttural mouth–twisting it often requires can be empowering and can make anyone easily sound *not* to be trifled with. I admit to using this well, even with my bad German.

"*Ich habe DAS!*" I said to a *Rewe* supermarket check–out *Frau*, thrusting in front of her a fistful of coins when, following six attempts to pay for my shopping with change, she was still unhappy with the combination I was giving her. Challenge many Germans (particularly Berliners) with even greater rudeness, in their own language, and they go to water … *oder Wasser.*

So perhaps speaking German and expressing anger in it, connects with the inner grump — or outer grump — in me. Annoy me long enough and I snarl equally well in either language.

But this doesn't work for everyone.

While recently back living / staying / killing time / enjoying northern summer in Berlin, a friend — Michael, also an English language teacher — complained about the unwillingness of his students to pay him any attention when he was teaching them. He said he had even become very annoyed and admonished the class in German.

Michael talked about this during a private German language class we had every Saturday with Torsten, a German language tutor. Torsten asked Michael what he had said in admonishment. I cannot recall exactly what Michael's words were, but despite their correctness, they sounded quite unconvincing. And Torsten – so German! – told Michael this.

To me, while Michael showed clear annoyance when he spoke, he did lack moral authority.

Torsten then asked him to say the same thing again, but in English. Michael obliged, and again he was unconvincing.

Laughing, Torsten said he would have laughed along with the other students, whatever language.

I then said the same admonishment Michael had made, only in English, but deep and purposeful and resonating. And then in German too.

And Torsten said, "Ah, you I would take notice of."

"Oh, that's just acting," I assured Michael. And to them both I said, "I'm just an old ham."

"You're a what?" Torsten asked.

And thus began my explanation of the meaning of 'old ham'.

Brot und Käse

~

They sat at the other end of the long bench, confident in their surroundings, standing up to scrape their backpacks off their backs, looking down the track, talking to each other.

I glanced down at the timetable I had taken from the Deutsche Bahn office inside the station building. The black and red numbers and names were ordered in neat columns and rows, as I had come to expect, but the train routes with different names and symbols were not so simple for me. I wanted to get to Göttingen – about a thirty–minute trip – where I planned to spend the day shopping and wandering like a tourist.

And looking at the timetable in my lap, I kept reassuring myself that yes, the train would arrive soon. But already dark blue local trains had arrived that were not on the timetable – not red or silver or grey national and international trains which, of course, would have no reason for having their numbers and destinations featured on a timetable for local services in the greater Göttingen area – but dark blue local trains, two carriages long, that *did* service the area. Yes, I was sitting on the right platform, in the right section, according to the timetable. But still, things can change, and I'd had enough experience living in Germany by then to know that you're only given the right answer when you know the right question.

Sitting there in the chilly morning, wearing shorts as I am

always hopeful it will turn sunny, I hoped I did not look as panicked as I tried not to feel.

I turned to watch the two at the other end of the bench, a brother and sister, she about twelve and he about ten, tall and blond in that way we think is German and is, but also isn't. He was unzipping his backpack, despite his sister's vocal protests, and pulling out a plastic bag. Opening the ziplock, he dipped his hand inside and gently pulled out a sandwich.

The sister told him – *auf Deutsch* – that he shouldn't eat it. But like so many younger brothers, he turned away from her, looked at his sandwich, and bit into it.

It was a very German sandwich, just cheese (very yellow cheese – *sehr gelber Käse*) between slices of dark bread (*dunkles Brot*). We often think German bread is far too dense, too much, too thick, the kind that, when it grows stale, you can take an electric knife to and carve it up for doorstops.

But actually, the bread is sliced quite thinly, far thinner than we know, so it's easy to manage and not too much at all. We visitors from the Anglo world get it wrong.

I could see two other sandwiches still inside the ziplock bag – exactly the same *gelber Käse*, exactly the same *dunkles Brot* – and zipping the bag up again, he gently munched on the one he had taken out, while talking to his sister with his mouth full.

I wasn't really listening to what they said. I was just watching this blond German kid eating a very German sandwich prepared probably by his Mutti or Vati or Oma.

I don't know if they knew I was watching them, and I don't know if they would have cared. It was just the three of us waiting for the train to Göttingen, and him eating the sandwich now at 11.15 a.m. probably because he was bored. Perhaps his sister was telling him again not to eat it – as big sisters can nag – but he ignored her and went on munching regardless. He had two more for later anyway.

The moment was probably lost on them. But it wasn't lost on me.

Bring a Book

~

In June 2008 I went to live in Hamburg for what turned out to be six months, four of them living in a ground floor flat in Altona, wedged between the adult entertainment district of the Reeperbahn and the River Elbe. I found much of it a very lonely experience. I taught English Monday to Thursday, and often went away on a weekend trip early Friday morning, returning late on Sunday. But sometimes – and I would truly dread these weekends – I would stay in Hamburg.

Saturday 25th October 2008

It would be great if next door to every restaurant, there was a 24 hour dental surgery. Then you could sneak in and grab a few magazines to read if you're unfortunate enough to be dining alone.

Reading makes you look busy when you are eating alone ... even if unconvincing.

On the way to Altona Bahnhof from my flat, I pass a number of restaurants and cafés: Italian then Spanish, then Italian again, then cross Max–Brauer–Allee to pass Portuguese, Indian, Italian, African and lastly, Turkish.

It was to the Turkish restaurant I went last night.

The restaurant must be quite well–known because people I know who don't live anywhere near Altona have happily said they have eaten there. It's often busy at night, and the noise of many customers having a good time struck me as soon as I opened the door.

"Table for one, please," I said, in German, to a very Turkish–looking waiter, dark hair and closely–knitted eyebrows. Looking at him, he seemed very preoccupied, and I have to say, I wished he was better–looking.

His head swivelled around the restaurant, and he said, *I think* he said, that the restaurant was full. But then he walked off around the corner, and not knowing just what he was doing or exactly what he had said, given language difficulties and the noise level, I followed him.

He then turned and said something that, while I still couldn't make out the exact words, was obviously, *no, no, no, we're full.*

I shrugged my shoulders and started walking towards the door, hoping I didn't look too foolish, when a customer – initially, I thought he was one of the staff – gestured that his table, freshly vacated, was available. He was by himself, I think, and perhaps recognised someone else who wanted to look desperately like it was okay to be there alone.

(Maybe when we dine alone we grin and grimace too much, all at the same time. Clutching the book we are reading like it's our only friend.

There is only one thing worse than eating in a restaurant by yourself, and that is eating your own cooking by yourself. Especially if you don't like your own cooking.)

So I sat at this table (for two), my order was taken, my yellow (!) Fanta was presented and I opened my book. The table next to me (mum and dad and two kids) paid their bill and left, and then another couple, young–ish (well, younger than me) sat in their place.

Then another waiter approached my table.

104

"Could you please sit at this table?" the waiter asked, indicating a move across the narrow aisle to yet another table. "Four more guests are coming," he said, meaning to join the young—ish couple.

"Of course," I said.

The couple thanked me, and I moved and opened my book again.

It wasn't until my meal came (no. 20 – *Nummer zwanzig* – on the menu, and a lot of food) that I realised the man at the table next to me (on the other side) was also alone. We were both sitting on the same side of our tables, so both facing towards the open kitchen, though I was reading and he wasn't. I wondered who looked the sadder.

I had clearly come prepared, *expecting* to be alone. I had a book which clearly did not fit in my bag, so I *must* have intended bringing it. Whereas he had nothing except the menu to look at, and the distance to stare into.

Perhaps we could have had a conversation.

Though maybe by *not* having a book he looked like he was expecting someone else to join him. So does that mean he was not as sad a sight as I was ... or more of one?

Of course I have no idea what his English was like. Maybe we could have had a conversation in German, if he had done most of the talking.

In between turning pages while I ate, I looked at the cutlery stamped with the restaurant's name in the handles (downmarket IKEA), and the plates stamped with the restaurant's name (green on yellow, around the edge) and thought that the restaurant was probably the swankiest Turkish eating place in Hamburg I had seen. Which, actually, is not saying much.

Eating by yourself is no fun. You can feel the stares (and non—existent stares) of others feeling sorry for you. (I do the same when I see others dining alone, and I am with company.) But in a popular restaurant on a busy Friday night you can lose yourself in the noise and the bustle and the food. And your book, if you have one.

The man at the table next to me left and soon after I was finished too, knife and fork placed on the plate in the way I understand to mean *I am finished and yes, I am well–mannered and cultured enough to know this is the way you show you have finished your meal.*

So I got up to leave, having paid (*Ich möchte bitte zahlen*), and as I put on my jumper and light rain coat, grabbed my umbrella, put my wallet in my bag and picked up my book, another man sat down at the table next to me.

By himself.

He looked like he had a glass of milk, though I think it was some kind of yoghurt drink. He was easily 10, 15 years younger than me and I thought, hmmm, wonder how many more meals he will have by himself. Bring a book, I wanted to tell him.

As I walked through the door to leave I had to wend my way through a crowd waiting for tables. None of them looked like they were by themselves. None of them had books either. But somehow the noise of the patrons and the hectic kitchen action made me glad I had at least been part of it, if only for a short time, the time it took to eat my *Nummer zwanzig.*

Because there was no way I was going to linger at my table afterwards: that would have made me look truly sad.

Acknowledgements

~

All but one of the stories in this anthology has been previously published. Thanks to all the editors and decision—makers who showed faith and interest in my work. Listed below are the websites where this work has been featured, so my thanks also go to: Christopher Allen, Walter Bjorkman, Cormac Brown, John Wentworth Chapin, Sheldon Lee Compton, Allie Dresser, Michelle Elvy, Frank Hinton, Len Kuntz, Jo McClelland, Gloria Mindock, Karen Eileen Sikola, Susan Tepper, Meg Tuite and Robert Vaughan.

Kitchen Scrap
A—Minor
http://aminormagazine.com/

Dotting every 'i'
Connotation Press
http://connotationpress.com/

A smile is worth 1000 teeth
Fictionaut
http://www.fictionaut.com/

Arrivals, Berniece, Big Dipper, Body to Go, Bus, The Deepest Cut, Dishwasher, First, Love, der Morgenmuffel, Verboten and *Write*
52 / 250 A Year of Flash
http://52250flash.wordpress.com/

Rainbow
Flash Fiction Friday
http://www.flashfictionfriday.com/

Always Vera and *Goose, and not turkey or duck*
The Glass Coin
http://theglasscoin.com/

Meeting Adjourned
Gloom Cupboard
http://gloomcupboard.com/

Monthly Coffee
Istanbul Literary Review
http://www.ilrmagazine.net/

I Swear and *Jacqueline Bisset and Me*
Language / Place blog carnival
http://www.blueprintreview.de/lap.htm

Snack and *Sydney Hotel Room*
Metazen
http://www.metazen.ca/

Bring a Book and *A Free Rinse*
Pure Slush
http://pureslush.webs.com/

Arms Width
Thunderclap Press (Thunderclap Six)
http://thunderclappress.com/

Brot und Käse
TrainWrite
http://trainwrite.tumblr.com/

Old haggis and *Lint*
Wilderness House Literary Review
http://www.whlreview.com/

About the Author

~

Matt Potter lives in Adelaide, South Australia.

Sometimes he works as a social worker, but more recently, he has worked as an English as a Second Language teacher, a job he loves.

He also works as the editor of *Pure Slush*, which you can find here: *http://pureslush.webs.com/* ... and you can find Matt's website here: *http://mattcpotter.webs.com/*

Vestal Aversion – a title he thought up himself, which was then slightly modified by his partner, who suggested the extra 'a' – is his first book.

Other books from *Pure Slush*

Visit the *Pure Slush* Store online:
http://pureslush.webs.com/store.htm

Many Fish to Fry
by Abha Iyengar
ISBN: 978-1-925101-59-1

The Company of Men
by Luisa Brenta
ISBN: 978-1-925101-06-5

The Vixen Scream
by Nancy Stohlman
ISBN: 978-1-925101-11-9

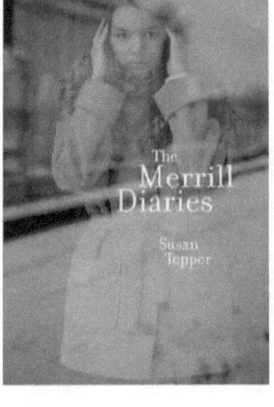

The Merrill Diaries
by Susan Tepper
ISBN: 978-0-9922778-2-6

itch
by Gary Percesepe
ISBN: 978-1-925101-21-8

Hard
by Dusty-Anne Rhodes
ISBN: 978-1-925101-80-5

www.ingramcontent.com/pod-product-compliance
Lightning Source LLC
Chambersburg PA
CBHW031843170626
46807CB00004B/1598